MAR/CH

Naughty!

Caroline Castle & Sam Childs

HUTCHINSON

London Sydney Auckland Johannesburg

One afternoon when the sun
began to sink in the sky,
Big Zeb called Little Zeb
to the banana tree.
'Time for bed,
Gorgeous,' she said.
'Cuddle up.'

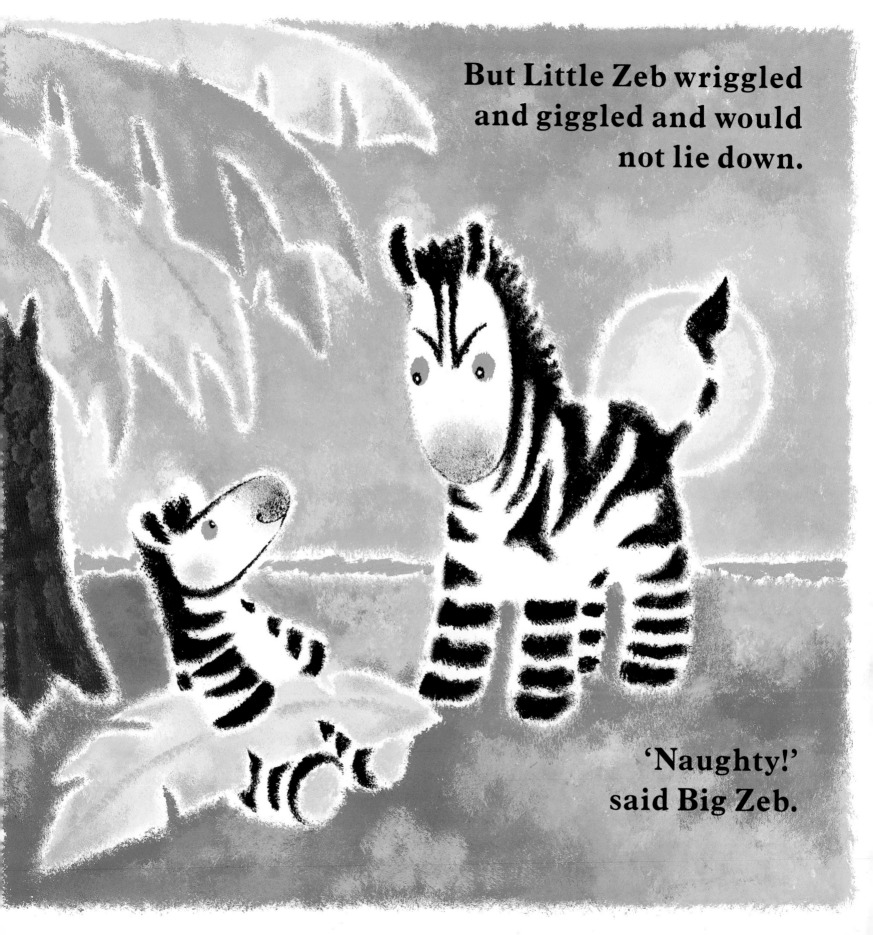

But Little Zeb wriggled
and giggled and would
not lie down.

'Naughty!'
said Big Zeb.

Little Zeb was not tired.
He threw off his covers and
made a loud noise like an
elephant's trumpet.
'Naughty!' said
Big Zeb.

Big Zeb decided to teach Little Zeb some games to
make him tired.

They played...

They played...

Whoops-a-daisy!

**Then, as the sun sank lower
in the sky they played...**

Hush-a-bye.

'There,' said Big Zeb. 'There's a sleepy Little Zeb.'
'Where!' cried Little Zeb. 'Where's
a sleepy Zeb?'

'You are,' said Big Zeb dreamily.
'You are my sleepy Little Zeb.'
'Not!' growled Little Zeb.
'Naughty!' said Big Zeb.
And she covered him
up in his blanket
and licked behind
his ear.

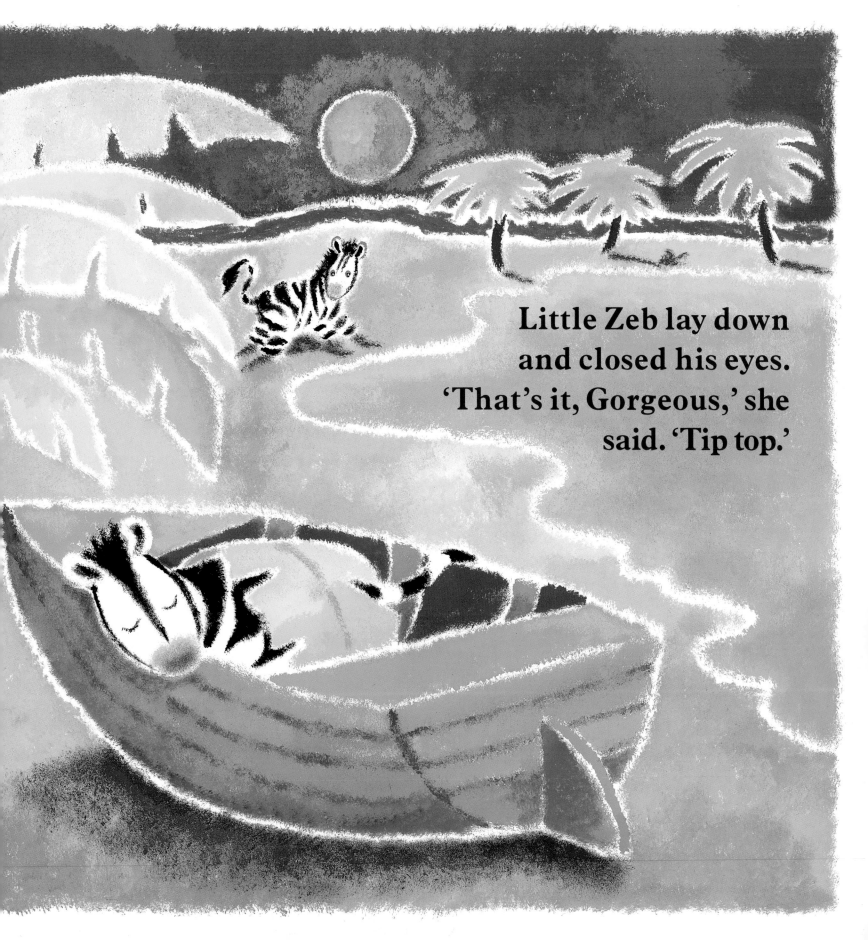

Little Zeb lay down
and closed his eyes.
'That's it, Gorgeous,' she
said. 'Tip top.'

But...

'Peek-a-boo!'

'Peek-a-boo!'

'Hey, peek-a-boo!'

Little Zeb made a splash
with his hooves.

At once...

two ears appeared
above the water...

then a nose...

then a great, grey wrinkly face which opened its
mouth and made a glub-glub wallowing sound.

'Peek-a-booOOOOOO to you, too!' cried Little Hippo. And he opened his snozzle and snorted a great big fountain at Little Zeb.

'Oooooooo, you naughty!'
cried Little Zeb.
And he splashed
Little Hippo
right back.

Splish!

All of a sudden, the water swirled around in a whirlpool. And from the water rose...

'Whoops-a-daisy!

A big naughty!'

Big Zeb was there
in a flash.

'What's all this splashing?' she said
to Little Zeb. 'You should be in bed.'

'What's all this noise?' said Big Hippo
to Little Hippo. 'You should be in bed.'

'But we're playing,' said Little Hippo.
'Tip top playing,' said Little Zeb happily.

**Little Zeb would not go to bed without Little Hippo.
Little Hippo would not go to bed without Little Zeb.**

So Big Zeb and Big Hippo wrapped them up
together under the banana tree.
'Hush-a-bye,' whispered Little Zeb.
'Cuddle up.'

As the sun sank even lower in the sky, Big Zeb and
Big Hippo looked at their sleeping babies.

'Who would have thought those two naughties could look so...'

'Gorgeous!' finished Big Zeb.
But...

'Peek-a-boo!' cried Little Hippo.
'Oooo,' cried Little Zeb in delight.
'Tip top naughty!'

For Alison Sage, with love - C.C.
For Francesca Forte, with love - S.C.

First published in 2000

1 3 5 7 9 10 8 6 4 2

© Text Caroline Castle 2000
© Illustrations Sam Childs 2000

Caroline Castle and Sam Childs have asserted their right under
the Copyright, Designs and Patents Act, 1988, to be identified
as the author and illustrator of this work

First published in the United Kingdom in 2000 by
Hutchinson Children's Books
The Random House Group Limited
20 Vauxhall Bridge Road, London SW1V 2SA

Random House Australia (Pty) Limited
20 Alfred Street, Milsons Point, Sydney
New South Wales 2061, Australia

Random House New Zealand Limited
18 Poland Road, Glenfield
Auckland 10, New Zealand

Random House South Africa (Pty) Limited
Endulini, 5A Jubilee Road, Parktown 2193, South Africa

The Random House Group Limited Reg. No. 954009

www.randomhouse.co.uk

A CIP catalogue record for this book is available from
the British Library

ISBN: 0 09 176977 9

Printed in Hong Kong by Midas Printing Limited